For Aria and Milo, you teach me how to be brave every day! —E.T.B.

To all of you brave enough to hold a pencil and create, the world needs you. Don't stop, give it all you got. —J.M.

Text copyright © 2024 by Ethan T. Berlin
Illustrations copyright © 2024 by Jimbo Matison
All rights reserved. Copying or digitizing this book for storage, display, or distribution in any other medium is strictly prohibited.

For information about permission to reproduce selections from this book, please contact permissions@astrapublishinghouse.com.

An imprint of Astra Books for Young Readers, a division of Astra Publishing House
astrapublishinghouse.com
Printed in China

ISBN: 978-1-6626-4064-3 (hc)
ISBN: 978-1-6626-4065-0 (eBook)
Library of Congress Control Number: 2023947898

First edition

10 9 8 7 6 5 4 3 2 1

Design by Melia Parsloe
The text is set in Wonder.
The illustrations are done digitally.

HOW TO DRAW

**Story by
Ethan T.
Berlin**

**Drawn by
Jimbo
Matison**

A BRAVE CHICKEN

Hippo Park

Chickens are known for being ... well ... chicken,
but follow these simple directions and you can draw a brave chicken.

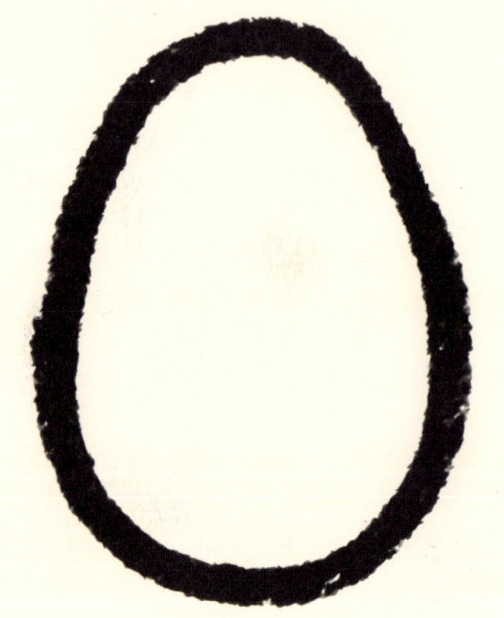

First, draw an oval.

Next, draw two dots for eyes and two triangles for a beak.

Then, add some legs and a curvy thing on her head.

Finally, give her some wings, add some color, and . . .

Um, wait, where's the chicken?

Oh, there she is!
She doesn't look very brave.
I wonder what will help?

I know! Knights are brave.
Draw her a suit of armor and a mighty steed!

Good job!

She looks so **brave!**

I bet she could fight a dragon!

Draw a dragon.

Okay, what makes me feel brave?
Oh! Draw her some friends and a trampoline!

Yay!

Good job!
Chicken looks so brave!

Maybe a little **TOO** brave.
Chicken wants to catch the dragon.

Chicken, it's great you're feeling so brave, but a flightless bird in a rocket chasing a dragon sounds like

a real bad idea.

Draw a rocket.

First, the body.

Add a line and a circle for the window.

Then, two triangles for wings and a rectangle on the bottom.

Finally, draw some flames to make it **GO!**

**And now she's not.
They've crashed on the moon!**

And the dragon looks...

HUNGRY!

Quick!

Chicken wants you to draw an ice cream truck...

Yaaay! Chicken, that was so **brave!**

But how are you going to get back to Earth?

Draw a waterslide.

Chicken wants to celebrate how brave she is!

Draw the scariest party ever, with fuzzy spiders, gross veggies, bike riding, singing in public, creepy clowns, scary ghosts, giant sharks . . .

...and accidentally farting at school!

But now Dog is scared.